*Featuring Jim Henson's Sesame Street Muppets*

A SESAME STREET / GOLDEN PRESS BOOK

Published by Western Publishing Company, Inc. in conjunction with Children's Television Workshop.

© 1984 Children's Television Workshop. Muppet characters © 1984 Muppets, Inc. All rights reserved. Printed in the U.S.A. by Western Publishing Company, Inc. No part of this book may be reproduced or copied in any form without written permission from the publisher. Sesame Street®, the Sesame Street sign, and Sesame Street A GROWING-UP BOOK are trademarks and service marks of Children's Television Workshop. GOLDEN®, GOLDEN & DESIGN®, GOLDEN PRESS®, and A GOLDEN BOOK® are trademarks of Western Publishing Company, Inc. Library of Congress Catalog Card Number: 83-83280 ISBN 0-307-12011-2/ISBN 0-307-62111-1 (lib. bdg.)

KLMNOPQRST

CTW
SESAME STREET®
A GROWING-UP BOOK™

# A Baby Sister
# for Herry

By Emily Perl Kingsley ✿ Illustrated by Richard Walz

TAXI

The day after Herry's baby sister was born, he went to visit Mommy in the hospital.

"Would you like to see the new baby?" she asked.

Mommy and Daddy took Herry to the nursery for all the newborn babies. A nurse held up a tiny baby monster. "This is your little sister," said Mommy.

A couple of days later it was time to bring the new baby home.

"It's so nice to be home," said Mommy.

"Herry," said Daddy, "what do you think about 'Flossie' for the baby's name?"

"It's okay, I guess," said Herry.

That afternoon Herry was playing fire engine.

"RRRRrrrreeee-OOOOoooowwww!" screamed the fire engine as it raced across the floor.

"Waaaaah!" screamed the baby from the bedroom.

"Herry," said Mommy, "please play fire engine in your own room. Your siren woke up Flossie, and she needs to take a nap."

When the baby had grown a little bigger Herry
wanted her to play with him.

"Hey Flossie," he said, tossing up a ball, "want to play
catch?"

"Flossie's still too little to play catch," said Mommy.

"I thought that when I had a sister she would play
with me," said Herry.

"She will," said Mommy, "but not until she grows up
a little."

Herry and Daddy were putting together a puzzle one afternoon when the baby started to cry. Daddy looked at his watch. "Flossie is telling me that it's time for her applesauce," he said. "We'll have to finish our puzzle later, Herry."

That night, as Herry watched Mommy tuck Flossie in, he asked, "Wasn't that quilt on my bed when I was little?" "Yes," said Mommy. "And it was on my crib when I was a baby, too. Your grandmonster made it."

Every weekend friends and relatives came to see
Herry's baby sister.
They brought her presents and took pictures of her.

"Baby, baby," grumbled Herry. "Everybody talks about the baby. What's so great about a baby sister, anyway?

"She can't *do* anything.

"I can't do anything because she sleeps all the time.

"I have to share with her. And her crying gives me a headache!"

"Everything for that baby is *special!*
"She eats special foods.

"She wears diapers and
special little clothes.

"She has a special bathtub...

...and special new toys."

Herry decided to do things
Flossie's way. When it was
time for milk and cookies, he
poured his milk into a baby
bottle and drank from it.

He tried to swing
in the baby swing,
but he was too big.

He climbed into the playpen and played with Flossie's rattle. Then Herry began to cry. He cried until Mommy came out of the kitchen to see what was the matter.

"What's wrong, furry darling? Are you a baby monster today?" she asked. "Come here. I have something to show you."

Baby Herry

Baby's
bath

"You were as little as Flossie once!" Mommy told him as she took a book from the shelf. "This book is all about *you* when you were a baby."

Herry sat in Mommy's lap and she showed him his own baby pictures.

Herry's first step

That evening Daddy said, "Being a big brother is an important job, Herry. Would you like to learn to give the baby her bottle?"

Daddy showed Herry how to hold Flossie and feed her from the bottle.

In the morning Daddy showed Herry how to
dress Flossie in her hat and sweater and bootees to
go outside.

Herry learned how to do other things for the baby:
He fed her with a tiny spoon.

He helped sort and fold her clothes
after they were washed.

PUFFO

He made up lullabies and sang
them to her when
she went to sleep.

One day Herry invited all his friends to come and see his baby sister.

Herry showed Grover how to hold the baby and support her head with his arm.

He showed Ernie how to hold the bottle so that Flossie wouldn't drink any air with the milk.

He showed Cookie Monster how to make the baby
laugh.

"Gee, Herry," said Bert, "your baby sister looks exactly
like you."

"Do you really think so?" asked Herry proudly.

That afternoon Herry asked, "May I please take Flossie to the park?"

"That's a great idea," said Mommy.

So Herry and Mommy and Flossie went to the park, and Herry pushed the carriage.

When they reached the playground, Herry's friends came running to say hello to Flossie.

Mommy smiled and whispered to Herry, "On the way home, we'll buy an ice cream cone. The baby is much too young for ice cream, of course. But we're not, right?"

"Right!" answered Flossie's big brother.